*Go to www.ingoblum.com and get
a book for FREE!*

INGO BLUM

WHERE IS MY LITTLE CROCODILE?

Illustrated by Antonio Pahetti

Where is Charlie, my little crocodile?

He is not in the garden.

He is not in the tree.

He cannot climb.

He is not on the street.

The street is empty.

He is not in the restaurant.

Crocodiles are not allowed in restaurants.

He is not at the zoo.

Where could Charlie be?

Is he driving a car?

No!

Crocodiles cannot
drive cars.

Is he climbing the mountain?

That is too difficult for Charlie!

Is he sleeping by the river?

That`s cozy.

No! There he is! We found him!

Charlie sleeps in his bed.

Look, how tired he is!

Good Night!

Charlie the Crocodile

Coloring Book

More Reading and Coloring Fun

ISBN 978-1-982942-12-0

ISBN 978-1-982941-74-1

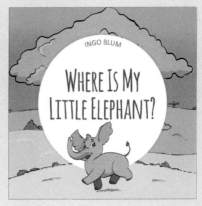

ISBN 978-1-982941-88-8

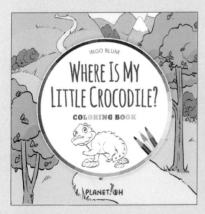

ISBN 978-3-947410-21-7

ISBN 978-3-947410-23-1

ISBN 978-3-947410-25-5

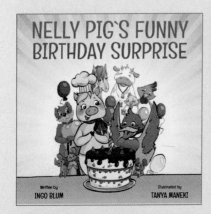

ISBN 978-1-983075-91-9

ISBN 978-1-982958-22-0

ISBN 978-3-947410-56-9

Thank You

Thank you for reading this little story. I hope you enjoyed it the same way I did while writing it. If you would like to know when my next book comes out, find more books I have written, and receive some occasional updates from me, just visit me on my website.

Do you find reader reviews helpful? If so, please spare a moment to help me by rating this book, so others will find it (and read it!), too. I always appreciate an honest review.

RATE NOW

Looking forward to your comments, reviews, and opinions.

About the Author

Ingo Blum is a German author and comedian. His journey to become a children's book author began during his day job. He has always enjoyed projects where he could create artwork for kids. He started writing stories to accompany these projects for fun, and with some encouragement from friends and family (and their kids!) he decided to share his stories with the world. Ingo works with international illustrators, with whom he constantly develops new concepts and stories.

About the Illustrator

Antonio Pahetti is a young artist with a lot of experience in children's illustration, who makes his illustrations with much love and a passion for details. His works are published in many countries. He lives in the Ukraine.

Made in the USA
Middletown, DE
13 August 2019